BOOKS BY DIANA O'HEHIR

Home Free 1988

The Bride Who Ran Away 1988

I Wish This War Were Over 1984

The Power to Change Geography 1979

Summoned 1976

HOME
FREE

HOME FREE

Diana O'Hehir

NEW YORK   *Atheneum*   1988

Thanks are due to the following magazines, in which poems have appeared: *California Quarterly:* "Artist's Model," "34,000 Feet"; *Field:* "Infant," "Hospital," "Pattern," "Questions and Answers," "Charlotte"; *Massachusetts Review:* "Your Face," "Shore"; *New Virginia Review:* "Home Free"; *Paris Review:* "Sleeping Pill"; *Poetry:* "My Father Owns This City," "Recognition," "Private Song," "Snow," "Lost Objects," "The Dead Pull Us Toward Winter," "Apple"; *Poetry Now:* "Meet Me"; *Poetry Northwest:* "Period Piece," "Payments," "Courtship," "Empty," "Under the Tin Roof," "Our World Ends in Radioactive Fire," "Firelight"; *Woman Poet—The West:* "Mosquitoes," "Recollecting the Tall House," "Waking"; *Yankee:* "Shells."

"Courtship," "Questions and Answers," "Payments," "Infant," and "Shore" were reprinted in *19 New American Poets of the Golden Gate*, ed. Philip Dow (Harcourt Brace Jovanovich, 1984).

An earlier version of this manuscript was a cowinner of the Poetry Society of America's Di Castagnola Award for a work in progress.

Copyright © 1988 by Diana O'Hehir

Atheneum
Macmillan Publishing Company
866 Third Avenue, New York, N.Y. 10022
Collier Macmillan Canada, Inc.

Library of Congress Cataloging-in-Publication Data
O'Hehir, Diana, 1929–
Home free.
I. Title.
PS3565.H4H6   1988   811'.54   88-19435
ISBN 0-689-11945-3
ISBN 0-689-70801-7 (pbk.)

Macmillan books are available at special discounts for bulk purchases for sales promotions, premiums, fund-raising, or educational use.
For details, contact:
Special Sales Director
Macmillan Publishing Company
866 Third Avenue
New York, N.Y. 10022

10 9 8 7 6 5 4 3 2 1

PRINTED IN THE UNITED STATES OF AMERICA

For

C.C.F.
W.E.F.
F.H.F.

Contents

I

II

III

IV

I

My Father Owns This City

. . . the rose-red city of Jaipur in India—
caption, *National Geographic*

I am telling lies to my two best friends.
They sit on cardboard boxes
Under the attic rafters,
Reading old *National Geographic*s, eating
Last year's chocolate Easter eggs.

Forty-two incised minaret spires
Against a pale blue sky,
That is my father's house, I say, that
Is my father's
Suncolored city.

Here is the rose-red man descending the stairs,
His shadow moves down the wall
The woman is in her red room,
The man stands over her,
Sunshine comes through in bloody filaments.

(Scraps of Easter egg melt onto my tongue)

And you can buy anything here:
A mermaid with pearl breasts,
Slices of the coral the city is made of,
A painting of me.

The streets of this city are warm under your bare feet.

Being inside this city is like being inside
Somebody's body.

Period Piece

My cousin Eddy and I lie on the living room rug
Halfway between incest and not.
It smells of kerosene and aniline dye. It is
Illegal in Kansas, not so in West Virginia. His dead mother and my
        dead mother,
Arms around each other's cinched waists, middy blouses pinned
        with safety pins,
Watch us from their other corner,

While the family bat walks up the roofslope with her big flat
        curving toes,
Squeaks, peers down the chimney,
The family secrets piled around us, two shoes, one stocking, one
        pair of panties, one
Cousin in the nuthouse.

A train hollers in the gully; claws
Skitter on the chimney flashing.
Eddy and I gasp, mouths locked. Our mothers adjust white cotton
        shirtwaists.
Eddy. We're waking the dead, we're
Astonishing our futures.
You're supposed to grow up and run a gas station, I to teach
        English; you'll
Die at 38, shot in the eye by your best friend;
This has got to stop.

Our mothers, touching each other's hair,
Are watching something beyond us.

Infant

The head tilts back, like a heavy leaf, the eyes sew shut
With a row of grains, the hand wavers under the chin, fingers
Splayed; this is
Exactly the way I remember it;
No syllable different; navy-blue
Boiled eyes, and cuckoo-mouth, cuckoo
Child; all of us always have known,
Recognition printed on the cells
Of the primitive body chart.

Every night that month I dreamed the baby was born,
It was fragile, creased like an overseas envelope; it was mislaid;
I had forgotten to feed it.
I woke up, moved my awkward belly into the bathroom,
Stood gasping at the edge of the washbasin. I would never
Be used to this.

And when I picked up the real baby it settled its heavy weight
    between my arm and my body.
Like a sullen beanbag,
Turned its face against me,
Pulled me into it.

Payments

That memory like a derelict plane
Appears on the horizon and steers straight at me,
Aged propellers clunking,
Motor spitting pieces;
I can't dodge it, forget it, run; I lie down flat,
Bury my nose in the grass,
It zooms over me, dropping rivets.
It doesn't have to hunt for me, it knows where I am,
I promised it something I never came through on.

An aged hospital:
Dirty rain outside, walls paved in fingerprints; on the bed
My child is dying; in the opposite wall
Is a window I'd like to jump out of.
I don't believe in God, but I try anyway: God in your creaking
      plane,
I'll do anything,
Reform, get poor, worship you,
Anything.

God hears.
The child is better.
He acts in a play,
Gives me a tin butterfly,
Falls in love, into debt, writes a poem
About salvation, grows up.

God in your fierce old plane,
This country understands perfectly,
We're waiting for the day raid, the night raid,
We know all about broken agreements;
Every scrap of disaster's your
Privilege.
Anything.

Political Murders

We fear for our children. We pull them in lucky from play. We
    fasten their seatbelts.

Digging into the past we find
That doubt still there, like a boulder of time
Blocking the present.
Days are chipped off, each one less than it ought to have been,
Cracked-opal days; fire spilled out of the fissure.

During one of those deaths, I was buying a dress.
The street outside washed itself empty; the mannequin turned like
    a clock.
I said, it wasn't that he was handsome, or polished, or young,
But lucky. He was really a lucky one.

Our wishes spread out in a newsreel of running;
And nights disfocus, tinny gaps between television stations;
Under our braced feet the miner
Lights his fuse; it climbs the air,
Dyes the night red as lost center of opal,

Lights up
A country made of mistakes, U-turns into
Deep diggings, with a view of two people hating.

Riding the San Francisco Train

Some day I'll go to San Francisco,
Climb on to the old red train,
Cross over the bridge to the far side,
And be different, simple, and plain.

Those shallow plain houses
Where nothing much ever happens,
Their panes of glass innocent as the back of a dog's eye.
People trudge upstairs in those houses, carrying wash.

Everyone knows his place,
God bubbles up through the evening beer,
The jukebox colors smell of candy,
The gold dust plant gets polished with car wax,
And God comes in again on the late movie,
Orders tomorrow's box lunch, orders no real pain,
Says put chocolate in the thermos.

I'll live there keeping my secret
Powerful as the magic grasshopper that creaked by the well.
No one will guess my true house:
Four floors of guilt, basement to attic,
Acres of garden, wet with confrontation,
Pain that goes stolid because everyone is thinking.

I'll live there, not ever thinking,
I'll have a son and a daughter,
Keeping my secret, until at seventy
I ride out to my own deep water.

Western Maryland

We printed purple leaflets in a gelatine-filled tray.

Purple in the roots of my fingernails, in my hair,
Purple streaks across our pillow.
Our landlady listened at the keyhole
While we made love in her purple-stained tin shower.
I was pregnant
And I thought in purple
Even though the three surrounding mountains,
Their coal-mine scars,
The boxcars halted at the crossing, the children
Who scrambled under them,
Were gray on gray.

McCarthy was in the headlines, you
Were the Party organizer.
I stared at my hectograph-etched hands,
The rim of color curving up my arm, into a place inside me,
Into my baby, still only as big as a finger.

I still think about that gelatine-filled tray,
Our message slowly sinking to the bottom,
The top of the gelatine firm, tensile, rubbery.

Brief Middle-Aged Affair

When I was 33 years old,
Skinny as a bedpost, nervous,
Red fingernails and red hair, I fell in love with Casey Jones.
He stood in the doorway, his hand in his bosom, grinning,
His cocked hat over his eye.

Darling, I told him,
You grin like my father;
I'll leave my husband for you.
My babies can grow up unaided; we can survive
On stolen peaches under a boxcar, on melted mud.

I said, Casey, do you believe in the flag?
It burst above us, a fever of blues;
The ailanthus sagged with our vision,
The ridge of the boxcar roof ate into my back.

And the orange-crate smell of a boxcar
Still makes me loving; truly I can't
Go into the hot valley at noon without seeing him,
His dark Irish hair in his eyes,

His wheels still traveling my dreams, traveling
More empires than Casey could build
Out of the dust
By the fern-bordered train track
Stroking me, coaxing me, bending me backward.

Recollecting the Tall House

Puts a cold hand on the belly of memory,
All those staircases to silence,
Landings angled over regret.

That house lives in a night world, stored under another pillow.

I'm awake now where hands and feet tingle rightly,
No jolt slams me flat through blankets
Back to the old neat prison
Behind the closet door which smells of linen;
I'm awake; I've forgotten it all.

The wizard who walks with me now is my own tame offering.
I can slit his throat; I can plant him like a petunia
Against the wall where the six revolutionists were shot,
He comes up a small neat houseplant, pale from the closet,

But with long pale roots. They probe the wall's foundation
Faceting inside of its rock another house,
A staircase, a closet,

A system echoing itself
Into the future,
Frame after frame, like the girl on the rainy salt carton.

Mosquitoes

Their language that high white whine that spans translation:
The insistence of your love losing momentum, of
My love drilling inward, of my VW swallowing a valve on
       Potrero Hill, of your heart machine
Drawing its outline of failure.

And the way they follow us, like memories, children, worries,
       guilt,
Criticism: *You will be*
Living off your father
When you're forty. Like mistakes: *I was too young. He was*
Too hopeful.

And how the bites linger on, old wrongs:
Scratch, apply cream,
Wake up at night,
I understand everything
Except for the way it ended.

Killing them, though, one of the few times
We master events. Not, *Does he love me, are they*
Talking, will they forgive, am I
Intruding, but
Finished. In a final smear of blood
Across the palm.

II

Staying Underwater Too Long

A hazard in deep-sea diving is "rapture of the deep," an
autohypnotic condition in which the diver is unwilling to
surface.

The danger for the diver is
A monster made of sea water.
It sings a song sweeter than a mockingbird's, swirls in the
    diver's skull
Seductively, blue like lobster claws;
Sand comes up over his toes, fish fidget his suit collar,
He lies down in the ooze; his body sinks slowly,
A jewel through oil; he's a headland, a crate,
The last word on his eyelids is color.

In London they rushed my husband through the morning streets
In a shrieking ambulance. He kept saying:
Nothing's the matter, smiled winsomely at the egg-crate roof,
Let me be. I'm so happy.
Dying felt good, I could tell; he liked the pull of it.
The 6 A.M. light washed promises into his damp round ears;
It smelled of old rags; it reeked of the cubbyhole under the
    basement stairs.

I tugged him up by his hair: Don't die.
The ambulance attendant gave me an English stare,
Jabbed with his needle. Far back in the pit of my husband's eye
    I could see
The monster draw itself back
Into its cave.

Recognition

The exact taste, tangy, somewhere between loquat and pear,
    why don't
We ever know it when we meet it?
No one says: Here's happiness' weather.

Three years from now or seven years we'll
Look at a photograph, the people small, communal as gnats, the
    house reduced
In sunshine, no ghost yet
Over anyone's shoulder, no stranger riding with a message from
    my mother,
Knocking all the ice plant off the slope
In his climb to our living room.

And we'll say: Happiness
Wasn't round or square.
It never named itself, was a series of negatives:
You were not inconstant, not sleepless,
I was not
Remembering things.

Hospital

Past the self-opening doors, the blond lobby with its caseful of
      dolls and flowers, rubber-sealed elevator, ward gate,
And once again I'm in the tan fear world
Where today you're a minor case in a patterned nightshirt and
      plastic drug dispenser stuck in your shoulder.
I kiss you.
We've been married twenty-five years next month.

In this hospital one of our children lay on his back for three
      weeks.
His jaw may not grow,
The doctor said. You almost died here. I
Almost died here.

And you tell me I've been too far away that whole time,
Fording these floors with their signs: *Slippery, Cautious, Walk
Carefully.* I talk at you in my hospital visiting voice:
The cat, weather, our children,

And you tell me I've been foundering
The whole time. No, I say, I was here, I was trying (*Visiting
Hours are over*), rowing down acres of reflecting hallway
Toward a patient whose hands examined
The metal rails of his bed.

Manuscript Decoded from a Lost Language

Down from the sky in balloons,
Gently,
Thousands of you,
You drift on to the yellow hillside, the bottoms of your baskets
        settle
Silently, with hesitation and shudder.
Someone says:
They've come to take over the city.

Your balloons are striped yellow and green,
The surface of the gas-filled bags silky in sun.

And we're as peaceful as cows,
Savoring the wild-oat stickers in our jeans,
The sun hot on the backs of our necks, the air motionless,
        creaking.

Why don't we scatter, fight, set fire to your armada?
Your moment seems a free gift from childhood
Pulling us toward a sentimental sky,
An arch of heat-sparkle;
And we're a holiday crowd, passive, warm, neighbors on a
        hillside.

We wait for the wicker baskets to settle forward,
For the leather doors to open, for something
To walk out among us.

Disintegrated Heavenly Body

I touch my planetary bracelet
Made from your dust:
Radioactive echo, reflected breath, nothing; it circles my wrist;
This band was friendship; here was trust, here
Regret, why did you have to end it that way, leave me not even
      my guilt,
Disappear into the vacant world, grab bag, over the edge of
Time, source, light.

From the wrong end of my telescope I watched you grow
      smaller.
Only a ring in the sky, you made a ring at my wrist
Marked opaquely, bands, years,

Pulling light to you, deadening it, invisible
Except in the quietest moment
Of starless night. Then

I remember,
Here, collapsed against my bone, this frail
Is the outline of a spent planet
Losing itself in itself.

Excavating

They were digging a pool in our backyard.

They brought in their iron bulldozer,
Raised its jointed arm above the house,
Gouged it down into the pale lawn, broke
The sprinkler system. Water spurted in arcs
Across the green sunlight.

You see life in metaphors, my husband said.
Nights, I dreamed of a heavy lake
Where I floated face down, arms and legs limp, breathing
Water. Daytime, there was the leaking red-earthed wound,
Dying grass, cracked cement, uprooted
Flowers, still blooming, upside down.

I put my hand under my bathrobe,
Felt the place where the nerves hadn't joined:
The memory of my body on a hospital table,
Tubes, fat mesh bandage, smell of blood,

And the insult where the knife forced itself in
And changed my breathing.

Your Suicide Has Let the Enemy In

There are places where we can't go; your body lies like a
       dropped coat
Across the low doorway; wind lifts your hair.

Outside, the barbarians lounge shoulder to shoulder,
They sum it up; their eyes say:
These are people who can't manage their war.

No message comes to our sullen world
Over the heads of those besiegers; their fur hats
Grow down across their faces, at the horizon's edge
Dust feelers spiral.
We're thirsty; your body
Tells us rest has forgotten us.
Your fingers curl splinters from the fortress floor
And the smelly army presses against the fence.

Are we the last city,
The only brown bump remaining on a caked world,
Sullied, forgotten, with your light body

Making an entryway for those hard wide skin-shod feet?

34,000 Feet

My body skips past the window,
Arcs itself, skinned naked,
Eyes chilled open, eyeshadow making crystals, wedged cold in a
       final question
How far is it,
All the way down?

Inside the plane my hand hasn't reached for you;
My shoulder doesn't stiffen on yours;
I'm a perfect lady, anglo-saxon, composed; I keep my dacron-
       slacked legs crossed,
I read *Time* Magazine by cubicle-light;
I have waked up two nuns.

While outside my death climbs the shell of the plane,
Leaves its trail on the window, X'd on the wings,
Frosts the drum of the motor, pursues
Me bone naked,
Fast past the window on my gymnast's circuit,
Leaving you, my former darling, former necessary, all things
Former,
Alone on your slipcovered seat,
Balancing last night's grudge, pressing your aghast to the
       glass—

She's out through the rubber-sealed window
Headlong down through the ice layer
Drilling her paper-doll hole in a shelf of cloud.

Private Song

The mockingbird
Repeats
Everything twice.

A slovenly builder, the mockingbird makes
A loose sled of twigs, bark, string, old package labels, old
Popsicle sticks, he glues this
To the lowest unsafe branches of the pine tree, he
Clutches the edge of this nest and sings

That although the moon's too low and whatever he builds
Too shallow . . .
Sometimes panic hits the mockingbird on his high note; he
      spins himself
Like a drunken gray and white top
All the way down the pine tree
Repeating
What he needs to believe.

I miss you when the moon is full; I can hardly remember you, I
      say it twice,
The second time is
For myself only.

III

Courtship

How I loved him.
With his damp white skin, his damp blue eyes, his
Tan hair stuck to his forehead in wet leaves,
His crepey fingers that found easily the fevers and suns of my
 body.
How I opened for him like an anemone, how I
Turned under him like sand, how the water came down,
Loud and black outside the window, how his cold phallus grew
 in my hand;
The ice shard in the gut,
The lizard mouth at the breast,
The black water blocking the door,
The rock coming loose at the fall's base,
Our hut melting, its reed spikes stuck together.

He's killing you, they called out. *Fight free.*
Who didn't understand the simplest thing about us:
His teeth marks like flowers, ridged fish chest, spiky brain with
 its webbed thoughts,
His world of drowning.

Over the fall we went.
Love soaked my lungs.
Across dark rocks, black sand,
We turned like logs,
I clutching him tightly
Even after they had pulled us up,
I shaking, entranced, head to foot in a scheme of bubbles,
And he with his bleached hands drifting;
He with his head swung back.

Empty

Every night since I left you I've been unfaithful
With anyone handy: God, a television voice, an airplane
      baggage checker
Who asked for my ticket and pulled me away from you,
And sent me through a waste of plane terminals, pushing a
      suitcase with my foot,
The light high and wet, unwashed;
It followed me into an empty hotel room with the heat too
      high,
And a frayed hotel magazine open to a page full of watches,
And loneliness
Folded into the quilted green spread.

And I lay down and closed my eyes and tried to retrieve you.
On the table beside the bed: an abandoned plastic shower hat.
And then I knew that I was unfaithful, entirely.
Behind my eyelids: nothing.

Inside my hand
Only my own dry skin.

Shells

Staying in other people's houses,
I'm afraid to open any door; it may
Show me the inside of the shell, the curved place,
The secret kept from sunlight.

But early in the morning at other people's houses
I'm lonely.
They're asleep, their breaths blowing on each other's eyelashes
        and foreheads; sea air
Wraps each of them in a blanket.
The beach curves, a hard pale shelf, edge to my life alone, tilting
        me off.

All the way across Long Island I saw the shells, molds of my
        fingers' ends in plaster,
The remains of an exhausted sea.

The animal has finished loving, it drifts away from its comforter,
The center is revealed.
The doors of its asking are open,
No muscle guards its threshold.

Meet Me

My grandmother used to sing that
In her vacant Maryland voice,
Cracked like a walnut:
If I don't see you again, this side-a Heaven,
Meet me,
That beautiful shore.

Dear Jesus, how I laughed; how I don't
Laugh that much now,
Missing you with that ache that's like a tooth,
Or a hole in the day, or no breakfast,
Carting it around all day: luggage,
And trying to remember your outline, and finding it fading.

Scene: Evening, that beautiful shore.
Shadows. Light supplied from above.
Out over the water a shaky pier.
And you in blue jeans and a plaid shirt
Have come down to the jetty to greet my brand-new body.

The hair on your arms is burned blond. You carry
Our supper
In a tan picnic basket.

I Search for My Mother,
Who Died When I Was Four

Every morning at two o'clock
I lean forward,
I go in feet first,
I let it swallow me

Into the catacomb of Knossos,
Through the tunnel that frets the world,
Through the deep aorta of the world's machine,
The open silent valve,
Its webbed fingers gray,

And there at the center you are, your hair fanned around you,
Your fingers spread on your shoulder.

In that heart of nothing my own heart stops.

Aren't you ever coming back? Can't you tell me
Any of your secrets?

But accident is a net of fabric around you.
You're a magnet for silence; it makes
Beads for the mesh on your coverlet.

Memory's hair is black.
The face of memory is carved from stone.
Nothing
Is memory's hallmark.

Our World Ends in Radioactive Fire

The city is poison, its metal roads
Poison, every quartz window
Enemy.
The grass withers our toenails yellow.

We stand on the edge of the remaining world.
Behind us, enormous carved city,
Its tops the square corners of storm waves.
That tallest enamelled roof
Scours the cloud with rays of sound: *Answer us.*

Yesterday they fused the city's doors; the fire inside burned
    clear.

Your hand reaches for mine,
You could be
Anybody.

Can you remember any fragment out of real life? The children
Posing like solemn actors on the lawn,
The underside of the porch roof painted blue?

In January, birds tumbled into our city,
Their wings frozen open.

Firelight

We closed the door behind us.
This is the last time in our lives, we said.
The fire flared up,
Hands reached out,
And briefly, there and then, we had it back.

Our youth like a great green jewel
Risen from the floor of the room,
Faceted, mobile, light moving and tumbling, possibility
Around us in a pool, unstable on the air like a
Holograph. I could see the chairs through it.

And all that while Time paced outside the door,
Cloth shrouding his elbows, long streamers of
Cloth down over his knuckles,
Silence silting into his hollow eyes,
A bandage
Locking his jaws together.

IV

VI

Shore

For my father

I remember, you tell me, a daughter, a love, as high as my
      kneecap.
That was me, I say.
You're 87 years old. We walk by the sea at Carmel.
You say: she slept in the upper berth of the train.

And now you forget me and I have to reach after you;
You're captious, like a plunging Japanese kite.

The ocean's harsh today, the wind's rising,
Our path lies along the edge of the cliff.
Hold my hand.

She had yellow hair, you say.
I know, Father. I love you
Because you're old, because you need me, because you look like
      someone I am forgetting.

Is his height like yours, does his head turn like yours, is he
Going to be dead, like you? Should I order us both a boat
For that long journey over daylight, up to the cold zone

Where you go when I ask a question,
Where the kite dips, dragging
Its long bright anxious chain.

Bedside

Waiting beside my father's bed, watching the pleated sleep, the
     small breathing,
The sheet is so clean and heavy,
It weighs more than my old father does.

My mother has come into the room,
She takes my hand in her young ghost's fingers,
She leans over the bed,
Her dark hair falls in her eyes.

My father's face is bony as a sparrow's body,
His nose pinched like the bird's tight legs, his eyes sculptured
     inside their
Blue eye circles, the forehead
In vine-blue veins.

Here he is now, Mother—
Your bright white husband, your day-warmer, your
World's perfect letter.

She touches a finger to his forehead,
Traces a branching vein
Her hair smells young and dark.

The Prayer Meeting at the Nursing Home

Blood of the Lamb, the lady preacher says.

The seven old ladies of the nursing home
Sing: *All my past in that mighty river*
That courses the hallways of our nursing home.

My father lies in his chair and holds my hand.

The seven old ladies testify what they're thankful for:
For a friend in Portland, sunlight, lunchtime, for Rajah, our lovely
Nursing home Siamese cat,
For the message God gave me on the mountain,
For the child
Who didn't die until she was three.

Mrs. Ross tells us that one. She's ninety-one.
Today's her birthday.
(Every day is Mrs. Ross's birthday.)

My father wakes and asks for the key to his other house.
(When we meet beside that water
All our troubles will be over.)

Blood of the Crown, shed just for me, the lady preacher says.

Lost Objects

Night after night I dream about my losses.
First, a topaz ring,
Second, the words of a promise,
Third, a revolution, fourth, a dollar in change, fifth, a canary
Stiff on the floor of his cage, his bird-fingers tensed into string.
Once, a house with a shingled roof,
A cat that lived in back of the house,
Two lemon trees where the cat is buried,
A view of the bay, a lover, a country,
Ten years of my life.

All of it pouring down the drain of a monstrous spillway,
Making a whirlpool, tugging at my chest, pulling my
Closed eyes oblong, my closed brain sullen.
The flood thumps in my forehead,
Pulls my hair, my bed, into its vortex
Over the rim of the funnel
Round and round like a cartwheel.

I'll struggle, I say. I'll grow extra fingers, grab, hold, salvage
Some of it, any of it:
My father's eyesight, my childhood talent,
The key to my house,
The short way home.

Danube Tour

The Milky Way was the dust of their horses;
In Hungary they founded the dynasty of the Arpads.

Every time I travel
I see men
Who look like my father.

On the river coast near Budapest
The Queen tolerated her brother to rape the beautiful
Clara of Zach; the family was tortured and exterminated;
Their castle transformed
Into a magnificent palace.

Upstairs on the sun deck the Germans play chess
With three-foot-high wooden figures,
And my father, hunched under his tweed jacket,
Explores the white-painted stanchions,
Feels them with knobbed fingers.

Clara's uncle tried to avenge her

I am watching my father, who is
Too close to the rail,
I am watching my husband
Who will leave me when this trip is over.

The Danube is only three feet deep at Budapest.
If I took my father by his bony hand
I could lead him very carefully,
Step by step, the water hardly attacking our shoes, almost
Dry-shod, to the other side.

Your Face

For my mother

The windshield of our car cracked in a spray,
Glass sprinkled the pavement,
Blood stained the face of my doll, filled one of her round
        cloth ears.
You went away.
I was entirely broken.

And I can't ever stop looking for you there,
With that ache in the weak left lung, the jaw line,
Or the end of a long corridor where I wait for you,
Four years old, in a white nightgown, calling out,
Help, or, A glass of water.
But when I see you there it's not what I've wanted to see:
You're leaning on the upright seat of our car
With me on your lap,
Your arm tight around me. But you are

Entirely changed, your eyes
Cracked across, your face
Shattered.

Pattern

My mother passed between me and the sun,
Her hair vapor and her eyes
Vapor and a mask
Of riddles over her face;
She revolved slowly,
Part of the procession at the cartwheel rim

Whose figures move faster than I do,
Shapes traced on air, forehead, brain pan, in
Appearances in unguarded places.
"Please draw the blinds," the stewardess says,

"Sunrise
In an hour."
And I tug at the textured curtain, see,
Scratched on the glass,
The tracing of my mother.

Strands.
Not a pattern at all.
People die when you're least ready.
In the railway station at Graz
My husband didn't recognize me;
He had turned me off like a light;
He'd walked away from the wreck.

"Coffee," the stewardess says, "tea,
And a vast space, rightside, under the wing."

If I could arrange that air,
Clean and balanced,
Jammed with dazzle;
But an outstretched hand goes right through it.

The Dead Pull Us Toward Winter

Her face with its scar, his with its
Childish American smile, are calling from December,
Always there behind the ragged summer bush, the magnolia with
      its last browning flower,
The dandelion heads spilt like gnats across the pond,
The grass hard as pine needles.

Years of other Augusts have ended the same way:
We spread our arms at the sky like statues of
Some discoverer, the sun pounds on us, the day is blue;
Where do we feel that doubt—(not in the ankles, the hollows
      under the ears)—
Their winter faces trying to be born again.

Without them the year would be hot pale summer,
The evening crickets so dense we'd feel our way along their
      clamor,
Sky streaked with sunset half the creaking night.

But his face and her face with their tan tightened skin and their
      eyes sewed shut . . .
Even in the height of summer
Their true world, clenched into itself
Draws our hot aimless days down, home.

Afternoon Nap in Carcassonne

The minute my head hits the pillow
I'm out. Towers, battlements, tourist shops, tourist busses
Fall down an echoing well. The clasp of
White stiff sheets, the smell of starch, that
Wallpaper flagrant with French roses; enclose me
In someone else's goodness; any stray
Outstretched palm come be
A mother to me.

Sleep well, Madame, the proprietress says; she pats my pillow
Professionally. I'm pulled
Straight through the earth's core. And here is the place where
My dead mother waits,
With her eyes
Out of an old photograph. I've found her.

When I wake up, Oh, my God, and where am I, all those roses
Blur against the wall,
While behind my forehead still, a woman's eyes, abstracted,
Like the saints' eyes we've climbed museum stairs to see
Day after day.

Questions and Answers

Who'll marry me? Cold Saturday. *Will he leave me?* With the
      blinds half pulled. *How will I*
Love him? Hastily. Now,
Can you finish your trip before dark?

You must go by the top of the hill, the bus, the bridge, the hedge,
      the bench,
There you'll be a child,
Your scrawny arms together,
Your hands clutching a pocketbook. You have a dime and a
      nickel. You're going
Down the road, across the town,
To the school, the store; you'll dance once across the supermarket
      parking lot,
Flare like a lighted pinecone,
Fade dull gray.

And there your coffin will be waiting, old lady.
Row it home
With your own two hands.

Now who'll marry me?
The green man with eyelashes of cornsilk, the tall boy with the
      dripping wet hair,
The lover with a valley full of wheat.

Home Free

Inch by inch along the bed,
Growing more compact, his arms pulled up like bird's wings
(My father is almost ninety),
I love you, I say over and over,
Until I read in *Time* Magazine that saying this holds the dying
      back;
They get polite, they hang around to thank you.
I love you, I say,
Under my breath.

In Bangkok you can buy a bird in front of the temple
For twenty cents. It's not to eat
Nor to listen to nor to admire but to
Set free.
Spring the door with your plastic diner's card, wait for the
      scrabble, the
Head poked out the door, air by your face,
And up he goes.

Snow

And so I pray: Get me out of this, God.
Turn my eyes north.
I climb into my car and drive toward the mountains.

This is exactly right. Drifts
Close over the car roof. Grains pack close, like a wall of lighted
      sugar.
Maybe I'll wait here forever. Maybe that's what I want.

I think of my mother, who died when I was four, of her hair
In desperate tangles spread on the air like anise,
Her mouth, dead pale, her gentle column of throat.

Mother, I'm older than you are now, old enough to be your
      mother;
Nothing's ever lost, is that right?

She presses her hands on the white glass,
Presses her pale young face, her fingers spread like flowers,
I lie back and watch the crystal lighted pane,
And wait for the machines and the people that are coming.

I touch my side of the window; it's
Not cold at all.

Charlotte

"You did right to hold fast to each other," I said, as if the monster-splinters were living things, and could hear me.—
Jane Eyre

The floors of our house
Are patterned like the cracked shiny face of the moon,
The wind comes under the doors and lifts the carpet.

My dead sister is a child of night, her heavy hair
Flung out on the dark two-o'clock sky, makes a scarf across the
        moon,
The tangled strands catch in the air's ice splinters,
Pull her cheekbones taut,
Her eyes open against the patterned sky,
She holds out her hand to me; our fingers touch.

I bank the fire in the study, sit down in front of it, and write my
        name.
I write, Yes, some kind of life is here.

You did well, I tell the people in my story,
To hold fast.

Sleeping Pill

And then the drug takes hold
And goes down into your arms and fingers
Wipes the pain along in front of it, washes
Cells clear. The white moons come back in your fingernails,
The bed unfreezes and cradles you; it becomes
That nest you remember from childhood, coaxed from a mat of
    leaves,
Wedged up close to the oak tree.
You lie there with your friend with the pale green eyes, the one
    who was shot in Vallejo.

He smells of dust and soap, there are shadows of leaf on his face;
    he props
Himself up on one freckled elbow;
The hot California day wraps you in its dry tart smell.

And now the drug drowns the base of your spine, it floats
A pale warm ocean around the base of the tree, drowns
The lover in his khaki pants; pulls you
Empty as a new boat,
Home.

Waking

They buried me in gold, stopped my mouth in copper,
Coated my chest with a turquoise bird,
Swaddled my thighs in a metal pouch,
Poured over me the lid of night,
Perfectly fitting, not heavy enough.

My bones kept saying: wake me;
Knit me back, slice off the tattered cloth;
Unclench my arms, stretch each one out;
The leather flesh will fill itself with life,
The light from the open door,
Fierce as claws,
Rake memory over the brain.

The knotted throat craves speech, the tongue bends for
A taste of basil, the eyes for
Red spinning candle margins, the rusty lungs echo:
I'm alive! Everything is still possible!

Inside my gold cupboard a bee is waiting,
Its wings poised over its back.

Apple

I examine the cut-open center with its darkly outlined
Double aura. Poking out of that is a seed, a small
Love point, a repetition
Of the pattern of sex.

This apple is symmetrical, with a neat curved stem.
The waxed outside the bright infertile green
Of artificial grass, the flesh
Bland, blank; molecules pressed so close
Their edges have merged.

But still, again and again, on all things growing, that pattern.

She stands naked in her garden, her red hair
Down over her shoulders, her freckled hand
Extended. Adam, she says . . .
Birds shift in the tree, turn
Their blue and scarlet tails under, leaves incline,
Each one spills a drop of moisture,
The small wind pauses, makes a bubble of stillness around
Her body, his body,
The apple green globe sits on her palm
All the light of steamy Paradise collects around it.

Adam bends his head. It's the world's perfume he's
Breathing in. It's the skin of that world
He sinks his teeth into.